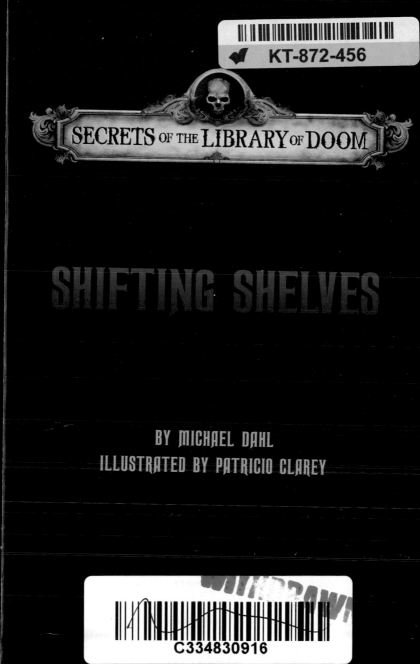

SECRETS OF THE LIBRARY OF DOOM

SHIFTING SHELVES

BY MICHAEL DAHL
ILLUSTRATED BY PATRICIO CLAREY

Raintree is an imprint of Capstone Global Library Limited, a company
incorporated in England and Wales having its registered office at 264
Banbury Road, Oxford, OX2 7DY – Registered company number:
6695582

www.raintree.co.uk
myorders@raintree.co.uk

Designed by Hilary Wacholz
Original illustrations © Capstone Global Library Limited 2023
Originated by Capstone Global Library Ltd

978 1 3982 3929 6

British Library Cataloguing in Publication Data
A full catalogue record for this book is available from the
British Library.

Printed and bound in China

CONTENTS

The Library of Doom is a hidden fortress.
It holds the world's largest collection
of strange and dangerous books.

Behold the Librarian. He defends the Library – and
the world – from super-villains, clever thieves
and fierce monsters. Many of his adventures
have remained secret. Now they can be told.

SECRET #6

WE MUST FIND THE PERFECT
PLACE FOR EVERY BOOK.

Chapter One

SECRETS IN THE SAND

A desert of red sand **STRETCHES** in every direction. It looks like an ocean of blood.

High above the desert flies a **DARK** figure.

It is the LIBRARIAN. He is on the hunt for a lost Page.

The Librarian looks out at the desert below him.

He hears a RUMBLE from deep under the dunes.

It is just as I thought, the Librarian thinks. *Turnus the Page is here.*

Like all Pages, Turnus works in the Library of Doom. He was last seen in the **OVERSIZED BOOKS** section before he went missing.

What evil brought Turnus to this dangerous place? the hero wonders.

He **DIVES** towards the red desert.

As the Librarian lands, the sand around him is **BLOWN** away.

Red clouds of sand fly off into the air.

FWWOOOOOOOOSSSHHH!

"The sand was hiding this," says the Librarian.

A stone door lies beneath his feet. A **LARGE** metal ring is fixed to the door.

The Librarian bends **DOWN** and tugs at the ring.

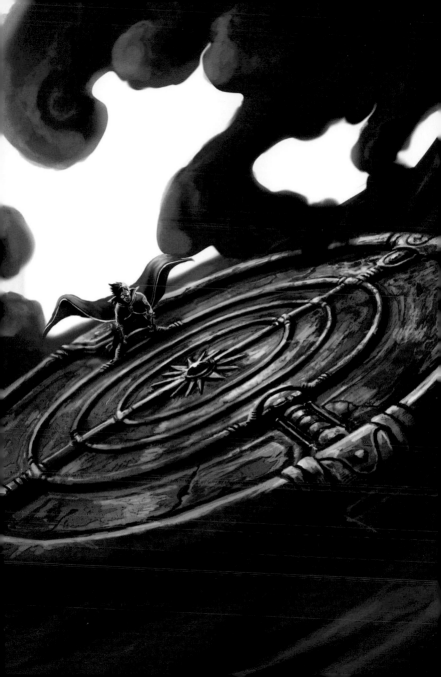

Chapter Two

BELOW THE STONES

The door **OPENS** up to a dark hole.

Inside, something large is moving and rumbling.

HOOM-BOOM-HOOM-BOOM!

The Librarian says, "I hope I am not too late."

He dives into the hole. He plunges into the booming **DARKNESS**.

Chapter Three

THE SHELVES

The Librarian's eyes adjust to the huge, **DARK** space.

Giant boards of wood **WHIRL** through the air. They twist and rise and fall.

The giant boards are the Shifting Shelves.

"Turnus!" **SHOUTS** the Librarian.

Uss-uss-uss-uss . . .

His voice echoes off the **MAZE** of moving shelves.

An **EVIL** wizard built the shelves more than one thousand years ago. They protected treasures that he stole from the Library of Doom.

After many years, the wizard and his loot were discovered.

The TREASURES were brought back to the Library.

But the empty shelves stayed behind. They are still full of **DARK** powers.

They will smash anyone who tries to leave the maze.

The Librarian **SHOUTS** into the darkness again. "Turnus!"

Uss-uss-uss-uss . . .

He does not hear anything except the echo. But he sees a red GLOW in the distance.

That shouldn't be here, thinks the Librarian.

The Shifting Shelves make it too **DANGEROUS** for the hero to fly.

He leaps from shelf to shelf instead.

The shelves **SWING** beneath his feet, but he is never thrown off balance.

The Librarian moves closer to the red glow.

Finally, the hero hears **ANOTHER** voice. "Librarian, over here!" it calls.

Then the hero sees a boy.

The boy is waving his arms for help. His legs are stuck in the cover of a **GIANT**, glowing red book.

"Turnus!" the Librarian says. He **LANDS** on the book's cover. "How did you get trapped here?"

"Look out!" the Page replies.

The hero and boy duck their heads.

FWOOOOOOSH!

The shelves **FLY** dangerously close.

"I was working with the **OVERSIZED** books," Turnus explains. "I did not know the book I picked up once belonged to the wizard!"

Chapter Four

THE WIZARD'S BOOK

Turnus says, "I started reading and–"

"You became **LOST** in the book," finishes the Librarian.

Turnus nods. "When I looked up from the pages, it had brought me here! My legs were **STUCK** in the cover."

"That book was **CURSED** by the wizard," says the Librarian. "His evil treasure always tries to return to the Shifting Shelves."

"How will we escape?" asks Turnus.

WHOMP!

A moving shelf KNOCKS into the red book before the Librarian can reply.

Turnus's legs are still stuck in the cover.
He does not get thrown off.

But the Librarian is **THROWN** into
space.

Chapter Five

REVERSE THE CURSE

The Librarian **TUMBLES** down through the darkness.

He lands on a shelf. But it begins to **SPIN** like a tornado.

The Librarian sees the glowing red book far above him.

He leaps off the spinning shelf. Its whirling movement shoots him up like a **CATAPULT**.

The Librarian **RUSHES** upwards.

He lands back on the glowing book.

"There is only one way to reverse the curse and escape," the Librarian tells Turnus. "We must _shift_ this book."

The Librarian **JUMPS** down to float next to the book. He grips it with both hands.

"Hold on!" he cries to the Page.

The Librarian starts pushing the book.

He **ZIGZAGS** through the air.

ZHOOOO-ZHOO-ZHOOOOOM

"What are you doing?" yells Turnus.

The hero **FLIES** them closer to one of the moving shelves.

He puts on a **BURST** of speed to catch up to it.

He puts the book onto the shelf. The wizard's book stops glowing.

Turnus's legs are now loose. He steps off the **GIANT** cover and stands next to the Librarian.

All around them, the shelves begin to line up. They make straight, solid rows.

The air becomes blurry. It grows **DARKER** and **DARKER**.

Then, everything becomes clear again.

The Librarian and Page are back in the Library of Doom.

"What happened?" asks Turnus.

"A book becomes a **GOOD** book in only two places," says the Librarian. "In your hands or on a shelf."

"The book is now back where it **BELONGS**," Turnus says with a smile.

The Librarian nods. "And so are we."

GLOSSARY

adjust get used to something

curse put an evil spell on something in order to harm others

dune hill of sand piled up by the wind

glow low but steady light

loot things that have been stolen

page young worker

plunge drop down from a high place

reverse undo something or cause it to stop

shift change places, positions or directions; also, to change into something else

wizard person who has many magical powers

zigzag move back and forth with sharp turns, such as in the shape of the letter Z

TALK ABOUT IT

1. What kind of dangers did the Librarian face in the Shifting Shelves? How did he overcome them?

2. Turnus was in trouble when he got lost in the cursed book. But getting lost in a good story can be fun. Have you ever read a book you liked so much that it felt like you couldn't put it down?

WRITE ABOUT IT

1. Imagine you are Turnus. Write about your time trapped in the shelves. How did it feel? How did you feel when the Librarian came?

2. Choose three words to describe the Librarian. Then write a sentence or two for each word, explaining why you chose it. Use examples from the story to support your answers.

ABOUT THE AUTHOR

Michael Dahl is an award-winning author of more than 200 books for young people. He especially likes to write scary or weird fiction. His latest series are the sci-fi adventure Escape from Planet Alcatraz and School Bus of Horrors. As a child, Michael spent lots of time in libraries. "The creepier, the better," he says. These days, besides writing, he likes travelling and hunting for the one, true door that leads to the Library of Doom.

ABOUT THE ILLUSTRATOR

Patricio Clarey was born in Argentina. He graduated in fine arts from the Martín A. Malharro School of Visual Arts, specializing in illustration and graphic design. Patricio currently lives in Barcelona, Spain, where he works as a freelance graphic designer and illustrator. He has created several comics and graphic novels, and his work has been featured in books and other publications.